BRATZ
Clued In!

Accessory to the
Crime

by Zoe Fishman

Grosset & Dunlap

GROSSET & DUNLAP
Published by the Penguin Group
Penguin Group (USA) Inc., 375 Hudson Street, New York, New York 10014, U.S.A.
Penguin Group (Canada), 90 Eglinton Avenue East, Suite 700, Toronto, Ontario,
Canada M4P 2Y3 (a division of Pearson Penguin Canada Inc.)
Penguin Books Ltd, 80 Strand, London WC2R 0RL, England
Penguin Ireland, 25 St Stephen's Green, Dublin 2, Ireland
(a division of Penguin Books Ltd)
Penguin Group (Australia), 250 Camberwell Road, Camberwell,
Victoria 3124, Australia (a division of Pearson Australia Group Pty Ltd)
Penguin Books India Pvt Ltd, 11 Community Centre, Panchsheel Park,
New Delhi – 110 017, India
Penguin Group (NZ), Cnr Airborne and Rosedale Roads, Albany,
Auckland 1310, New Zealand (a division of Pearson New Zealand Ltd)
Penguin Books (South Africa) (Pty) Ltd, 24 Sturdee Avenue,
Rosebank, Johannesburg 2196, South Africa

Penguin Books Ltd, Registered Offices:
80 Strand, London WC2R 0RL, England

 www.bratzpack.com

Used under license by Penguin Young Readers Group. Published in 2006 by Grosset & Dunlap, a division of Penguin Young Readers Group, 345 Hudson Street, New York, New York 10014. GROSSET & DUNLAP is a trademark of Penguin Group (USA) Inc. Printed in the U.S.A

Library of Congress Cataloging-in-Publication Data

Fishman, Zoe.
 Accessory to the crime / by Zoe Fishman.
  p. cm. — (Clued in! ; #4)
 "Bratz."
 ISBN 0-448-43966-2
 I. Title. II. Series.
 PZ7.F5358Acc 2006
 [Fic]
                    2005022180

10 9 8 7 6 5 4 3 2 1

BRATZ
Clued In!

Accessory to the
Crime

Chapter 1

"So, what can we do to make sure this is the most amazin' party of the year?" asked Cloe.

"You mean besides showing up and being our supercool selves?" joked Jade. Cloe tossed a throw pillow at her friend's head as they all giggled.

"Yes, *besides* that!" Cloe exclaimed.

Cloe, Jade, Sasha, and Yasmin were all gathered in Cloe's bedroom, trying to think up ideas for Cameron's birthday party. Cloe had been planning it for weeks—she had sent the invites out and had set Cameron's basement as the location. Now she just needed to come up with the perfect finishing touches to make sure Cameron's birthday party would be the bash of the year!

"What if we made a huge birthday card and had everybody sign it with special notes to Cameron?" asked Sasha.

"That's a great idea," agreed Cloe. She wanted Cameron to remember the party forever, and a supersized card was a souvenir he'd be sure not to lose.

"Sweet! I'll design it on my computer," said Sasha. "I know what a freak Cameron is for snowboarding, so maybe I'll Photoshop his head onto the body of a professional snowboarder!" She jumped up and pretended to be strapped to a board while careening down a slope, with her arms waving wildly.

"That's so funny!" said Cloe, laughing at Sasha's snowboarder imitation. "He'll love that."

Cloe stretched out on her lavender comforter. She picked up her stuffed monkey, Chiquita, and hugged her to her chest. "What should we do about the decorations?"

"Why don't we just do it old-school?" suggested Jade. "With streamers and balloons, plus Sasha's giant 'Happy Birthday' card. If we just stick to the basics, the basement will look great. We can save money, and the cleanup will be minimal."

"Sounds good to me," agreed Sasha. "I like it. Low-maintenance but stylin'."

"Just like us!" Cloe exclaimed as they all burst into uncontrollable giggles.

Cloe was excited about throwing a party for Cameron. She really liked organizing things, especially superfun events like birthday parties. It was important to her that Cameron have a great time because he was such a fantastic friend.

"So, we have the decorations down," Cloe said. "Now, what about refreshments?"

"Easy!" said Sasha. "We can make or buy all sorts of food and spread it out all fancy on a table."

"Yum!" said Yasmin. "I vote for sushi. I know this great restaurant that's pretty cheap, but the sushi is grade A. We could chip in and buy a couple of platters for hardly any money at all."

"Good call on the platters," said Cloe. "Because I know I have no idea how to make sushi. Talk about complicated!"

"We can stash soda and bottled water in huge coolers beside the refreshment table," added Sasha.

"And veggie trays plus chips and dip are always great for party snacking," Jade chimed in.

"Perfect!" Cloe exclaimed. "Sounds like an awesome menu to me! And I'll make my famous cupcakes for dessert."

"Mmm, this all sounds so good—I wish it were *my* birthday!" Yasmin blurted out.

"Don't worry, Yas," Cloe teased. "I'm sure if you ask nicely, Cam will share some of his birthday chow with you."

"Let's hope so!" Jade said with a laugh. "I'm gettin' hungry just thinking about the delish spread we're dreaming up!"

"Enough talk about food, girls," Sasha declared. "What about the most important party decision—what are we all going to wear?"

"Good question, Sasha!" Cloe exclaimed. "I can tell you've got something kickin' planned—so spill!"

"Well, I did just get this supercute denim miniskirt last weekend at the mall. It has these adorable heart-shaped back pockets. I was thinking about wearing it with that hot-pink T-shirt I have," said Sasha.

"Ooh, that's a great look," said Cloe.

"Okay, Jade, what's on your *fashion* plate?" The girls all cracked up at Cloe's pun.

When she caught her breath, Jade replied, "I've got this little green strapless dress I've been looking for an excuse to wear. I thought Cam's birthday would be the perfect occasion to strut out in something new!"

"Totally," Cloe agreed. "Okay, Pretty Princess, whatcha got?"

"I just snagged this hot little black ruffled skirt," Yasmin said. "I was planning to pair it with a strappy, sparkly gold top. What do you think?"

"I think we're all gonna look rockin'!" Cloe gushed.

"Um, hello, Cloe, fabulous party planner

of the universe," Sasha interrupted.
"What are *you* going to wear?"

"I'm actually not quite sure.
It has to be the perfect mix of casual and cool,
you know? I have this fuchsia-colored shrug that
looks great with my flowered halter top, but I
don't have a bag to match. I guess I could wear
my brown blazer, but it's just not as festive."

"No, wear the fuchsia one. You don't need
a bag," said Jade. "You can just put your stuff in
your pockets if you have to."

"Girl, every outfit needs its matching
purse—hello!" said Cloe, laughing. "Besides I'm
bringing Cameron's gift to the party, and I don't
want to carry it in a plastic bag. That would totally
destroy my look."

"Good call!" agreed Yasmin. "Okay, so you need a bag. Wait, hold on a second! A secret surprise present for Cameron? You've been holding out on us! What did you get him?"

"Yeah! Tell us!" squealed Sasha.

"You guys," said Cloe slyly, "it's a *surprise*."

"What is it? What is it? You have to tell us!" Jade yelled.

"Okay, but I'm not going to show you what I made, or tell you any details, because I want it to be a surprise to you, too," said Cloe. She was so excited about her gift for Cameron. She had really thought hard about what to get him. The gift had to be perfect—both a reflection of Cameron's personality and of what his friendship meant to Cloe. Just when she thought that she would never come up with the perfect idea, she had! She'd just been listening to the radio when the plan for an absolutely ideal gift hit her.

"You're killing us!" said Yasmin. "Tell us what it is right this very second!" She got up from the floor and jumped on the bed with Cloe. "Right now! Or Chiquita gets it!" Yasmin grabbed Chiquita and put him in a headlock.

"Okay, okay!" said Cloe, laughing. "I'm making him a CD of his favorite songs."

"That is so cool!" the girls exclaimed.

"It's not just any CD, though," added Cloe. "I'm including all of his absolute fave tunes for all different moods and occasions. I'm going to decorate the case and design personalized liner notes and everything. But you'll see it when I give it to him."

"I'm sure he's going to love it," said Sasha. "We can't wait to see it either!"

"For real!" said Yasmin. "Cloe, you are so creative—I'm sure it will be perfect."

"Thanks, guys," said Cloe. She hoped that Cameron would like it—and she *really* hoped the party would be a big success!

Chapter 2

The day of the party, Cloe spent all morning putting the finishing touches on Cameron's CD. She had already spent hours downloading his favorite songs and burning them onto his special birthday disc. And now she was personalizing the case with stickers and a homemade label that read "Happy B-day, Cam!" in glitter paint. Getting the glitter just right had taken hours, but she was so pleased with the result that it was totally worth it!

After she wrapped the CD, Cloe rounded up the girls and went over to Cameron's house early to set up for the party. They artfully draped streamers, hung balloons at just the right spots, and arranged the luscious spread of food and drinks on a big table, including the adorable vanilla and chocolate cupcakes Cloe had baked the night before. Each cupcake was iced with light blue frosting and had a letter on top, which, when arranged together, spelled out HAPPY BIRTHDAY CAMERON.

The final touch was the supersized birthday card, which they displayed prominently at the foot of the basement stairs. When they were finished, it looked awesome! Cloe could hardly contain her excitement—everything had come together so beautifully.

"Hey, Cloe, my basement looks so fly, I can't believe it's the same room!" said Cameron, smiling broadly as he walked down the stairs.

"Really? I'm happy you dig it, Cameron," Cloe replied. "I wanted to make it hip and colorful but, you know, not overdone. I'd call it 'bohemian chic.'"

"'Bohemian chic,' huh? I'm not so sure I know what that means, but everything looks kickin'. Thank you all for doing this," Cameron said.

Cloe smiled shyly. She was superpsyched. This was definitely going to be a party to remember.

"Hey, Cloe, could you hand me the CDs from the coffee table?" Sasha called from across the room.

"Sure, no sweat," Cloe called back. She grabbed the discs and walked them over to Sasha, who was making sure that only the sweetest, most dance-worthy tunes were on rotation.

"Cloe, you look so great!" Sasha whispered. Cloe glanced down at her outfit—a brand-new suede miniskirt and a flowered halter top underneath her fantastic fuchsia shrug. Her brown round-toe boots were fabulous, and she had twirled her hair up into the perfect slightly messy bun. "Wait, where's the bag you were so stressed about?"

"It would have been such a drag to carry it around all night, you know?" said Cloe. "You guys were totally right about the purse not mattering. I shopped and shopped until I found the perfect one and then I just ended up putting it in the closet with my coat. Can you believe it?" she said with a laugh.

"Girl, that's too funny," said Sasha.

"Hey, Cloe, did you make these cupcakes?" Cloe turned to find Felicia right behind her.

"Yes—do you like them?" Cloe asked.

"Are you kidding me?" Felicia said. "They look so yummy, and that lettering is way cool! How'd you get them to look so sweet?"

"Let's just say this isn't my first batch!" Cloe replied.

Felicia giggled. "Wow, that is dedication, girl! Do you mind if I eat one of the Y's?" she asked.

"*Why* not?" Cloe replied, and the girls burst into giggles.

As more guests arrived, Yasmin got up to

dance. Eitan, Valentina, and Kiana
were watching her carefully, trying
to follow her moves. "Girl, you really
know how to move!" Eitan yelled
over the music to Yasmin.

Yasmin laughed. "Thanks, Eitan!" she yelled
back.

"For real," Valentina chimed in. "I can barely
keep up!"

"Say cheese, y'all!" said Jade as she snapped a
photo with her digital camera.

"Lemme see, lemme see!" Kiana exclaimed. Jade
handed her the camera. "Ooh, my eyes are shut! Take
another one!"

"On the count of three, everyone say, 'Cameron!'"
Jade exclaimed as she snapped another shot.

Chapter 3

Cloe surveyed the scene. Even though the party was winding down, it was clear that everyone had had a great time. Dana and Cade were trying to cool off from all their dancing by fanning themselves with paper plates, and Jade and Yasmin were sharing the last piece of sushi. Cameron was busy making the rounds, thanking all the guests for coming.

Just then, Cloe noticed Kiana walking out with her coat slung over her arm. *That's strange*, Cloe thought. *Isn't Kiana going to say good-bye?*

"Hey, Kiana!" Cloe yelled. Kiana turned

around nervously to face Cloe.

"Oh, hi, Cloe," she said.

"Are you leaving?" asked Cloe.

"Oh, yeah, sorry, I, um ..." Cloe noticed that Kiana wouldn't look her in the eye. "I have to go," Kiana said hurriedly.

Cloe felt someone brush past her on her other side. She turned to see Cameron running by with a roll of paper towels.

"Hey, Kiana, hold on a sec," Cloe said. "Cameron, what's the matter? What's with the paper towels?"

"Somebody spilled soda on the couch. I just have to clean it up. It's no big deal," he said, giving her a quick smile before he rushed away.

Cloe turned back around, and Kiana was

making her way toward the door again. "Thanks for coming, Kiana!" Cloe called.

Kiana looked back at Cloe. "Oh, yeah, thanks for having me. Sorry I have to rush off!" Cloe was confused by Kiana's behavior. It wasn't like her to rush off without a proper good-bye.

Cloe checked her watch. The time really had flown. Maybe that was why Kiana was in such a hurry to leave. Cloe noticed other people checking their watches and moving toward the coat closet as well.

I'd better go get Cameron's gift, Cloe thought, and hurried over to the closet.

As she made her way to find her coat and bag, Cameron intercepted her. "Hey, Cloe," he said shyly.

"Hey, Cameron," she replied. "Did you have a good time?"

"Cloe, this was, like, the best party ever. It was so nice of you guys to throw it for me. Especially you," Cameron said.

"I'm so glad you had fun!" said Cloe, blushing a little.

"I really did. And those cupcakes—wow! Those are ridiculously good. I can't wait to have one for breakfast," said Cameron.

"Breakfast?" Cloe exclaimed. "You're crazy!"

They both laughed. "Hey, if cupcakes for breakfast makes you crazy," Cameron said, "then sign me up for the loony bin!"

"I guess we'll have no choice!" Cloe replied,

giggling at her friend's joke. "But before they take you away, I have something for you. Wait right here, okay?"

"What? Cloe! Come on, that's too much— this sizzlin' party is the coolest present I could've asked for!" said Cameron.

"Oh, please!" said Cloe. "It's your birthday— and since when did the girls and I ever mind throwing a party?"

Cloe approached the coat closet and pulled her lavender coat off the hanger, then reached down to the floor to retrieve her purse. *That's strange*, she thought. She had put her bag in the right corner of the closet, toward the back. She searched the entire closet. There was Yasmin's bag and Jade's bag and Sasha's bag—but where was hers? She felt herself starting to panic.

Jade came up behind her. "Is everything okay, Angel?" she asked.

"Jade, I think my purse is missing!" Cloe whispered.

"What? No way!" Jade said. "Where did you leave it?"

"Right in the corner, toward the back," Cloe replied.

"Well, maybe someone moved it while they were looking for their own bag," Jade suggested.

"That's what I figured, but it's not there! I searched the entire floor of the closet," replied Cloe nervously.

"Okay wait, let me look," said Jade. She got down on her hands and knees and searched the closet, but she couldn't find anything either. She stood up, biting her lip. "Cloe, you're right. It's not there! Are you sure this is where you left it?"

"I'm positive. This can't be happening!" Cloe cried. "I can't imagine where it went!" She felt close to tears. Not over the bag, although she loved it, but over what was inside the bag. She had worked so hard on Cameron's CD, and now she had nothing to show for it!

Sasha noticed the commotion and rushed over. "Angel, what's the matter?" she asked.

"Sasha, my purse has totally gone missing!" Cloe said.

"She left it right here in the coat closet," Jade explained. "There, in the right-hand corner by ours. We searched everywhere, but I dunno," Jade said as she shot a nervous glance at Cloe. "It seems to be gone." Hearing Jade confirm her fears made Cloe's eyes fill with tears.

"Oh, no. It's got to be somewhere!" Sasha said. "We'll find it—don't worry." Sasha rounded up the others and they searched every nook and cranny of the basement. She and Jade looked in the bathroom, Eitan searched behind the stereo with a flashlight, and Cameron even dug around inside the cooler. Cloe's bag was nowhere to be found.

"What would anybody want with my purse?" Cloe said as she tried to hold back her tears. "How could somebody *steal* from me?" She felt so sad and helpless.

Chapter 4

Jade, Cloe, Sasha, and Yasmin collapsed on the couch, finally giving up on their futile search.

"Oh, Angel, I'm so sorry," said Jade. "I can't believe your purse is missing. What was in it—I mean, besides the CD?"

"Nothing, really," Cloe sniffled. "Some money and my lip gloss. Luckily I stuffed my cell into my pocket, like you guys suggested." Cloe reached down to pat her pocket. The way this night was going, she couldn't be sure of anything without double-checking. Thankfully, her cell phone was there, right where she had left it.

"Well, that's not so bad," said Jade. "I know it stinks, but you can always reburn the CD, right?"

Jade was right, but Cloe was still bummed that she'd have to start all over again with the label and case design. She'd had it perfect, and now she was afraid she'd never get it exactly right again!

"Yeah, I guess so," Cloe sighed. "But I just bought that bag. I mean, just this week." She remembered finding the bag at the mall. It was made from this delicious-looking nubby gold leather. And it was the perfect size—roomy enough to hold a couple of essentials, but not too big to take to a party. The best part was its fringed strap. Cloe had been so excited because she had just seen something like it in her favorite fashion magazine.

"I know, girl," said Sasha. "I'm so bummed for you. Where did you get that purse, anyway? Was it expensive?"

"I got it at the mall," replied Cloe. "You know that new store Etc.? It wasn't *so* expensive, but I definitely had to dip into my savings."

Cameron, Eitan, and Cade sat with the girls on the couch. They all looked frustrated and tired.

"Geez, man, we looked everywhere," said Koby as he joined his friends in the basement. "This is so incredibly uncool."

"I know!" exclaimed Cameron. "At my

house, of all places. Cloe, I am so, so sorry." Cameron felt terrible that Cloe had been ripped off, especially after she'd gone to so much trouble to throw this party for him. Even though she made the planning seem so effortless, Cameron knew that she had spent a lot of time thinking through every detail.

"Guys, it's not your fault! I guess we just have to forget about it," said Cloe. She knew that dwelling on the purse would just drag everyone down. The last thing she wanted to do was ruin everyone else's night with her drama.

"No way!" said Yasmin. "I'm sorry, Cloe, and I hate to say this, but I really think your purse was stolen. Things don't just disappear. Unless somebody here is a magician, one of the guests must have totally walked off with it."

"Do you really think so?" asked Cade, puzzled. "I mean, I guess that is the only explanation. But who would do such a thing?"

"I'm not sure," said Yasmin as she put her arm protectively over Cloe's shoulder. "But I'm not gonna rest until I find out. Did you guys notice anyone hanging out by the coat closet or acting shady?"

"Hmmm, I don't think so," answered Jade. "I was too busy having a great time to really notice."

"Wait," said Cade. "Now that I think about it, I did see Kiana rummaging around in the closet for a while before she left. And then, once she had her things, she practically ran out of here."

"Oh, wow, you're right," agreed Cloe. "Kiana was acting really strangely before she left. She wouldn't have even said good-bye to me if I hadn't called her over. You don't think Kiana could have taken it, do you? What would she want with my purse, anyway?"

"Wow, I don't know, Cloe. But it certainly sounds like maybe she took it. I mean, otherwise, why would she rush out of here so quickly?" replied Jade.

"Okay, but how are we going to figure out whether or not Kiana has Cloe's purse without coming right out and asking her?" asked Sasha.

Everyone pondered this for a minute and then Jade piped up. "Wait, I have it. Here's what I'll do: I'll call Kiana in the morning and ask her if she had fun at the party. Then I'll listen for any signs that she's hiding something."

"Like a secret agent!" exclaimed Cade.

"Exactly!" agreed Jade. "And Cloe, after I talk to her, I'll call you with the scoop."

Cloe didn't like having to be so sneaky with Kiana, but she couldn't think of another option. She wanted her bag back, but more importantly, she wanted Cameron's CD back.

"Great idea, Jade," Cloe said. "It's a plan."

"Yeah!" whooped Eitan and Cameron.

Cloe laughed. It helped to know that her friends wouldn't rest until justice was served.

Chapter 5

Cloe woke up the next morning to the sound of her cell phone ringing.

It was Jade.

"Hi, Jade!" Cloe exclaimed.

"Mornin', honey," answered Jade. "How are you feeling?"

"Okay," said Cloe. "Did you talk to Kiana?"

"I did," said Jade. "And I think we might have our purse-stealer."

"Really?" Cloe exclaimed in disbelief. "No way. What did she say?"

"Meet me at the smoothie shop in an hour," said Jade. "I'll give you the full scoop."

"Right on," answered Cloe. She hung up and sighed. As encouraging as it was that Jade had found a lead, Cloe was still hurt by the thought that someone she knew and trusted would steal from her. She couldn't wait to get the full story from Jade.

At the smoothie shop, Cloe found Jade in a trench coat and sunglasses, reading a newspaper at a table by the door. Jade sure was taking her new role as detective seriously!

"So, Sherlock," Cloe said as she sat down across from Jade, "give it to me straight."

"Here's the deal," said Jade. "I called Kiana and she was all normal with me until I started asking her about the party last night."

"What do you mean?" asked Cloe.

"As soon as I asked her whether or not she had fun, she got kind of quiet and unresponsive," said Jade.

"Like how?" asked Cloe.

"She basically changed the subject and started talking about our Spanish test tomorrow," said Jade.

"Weird!" said Cloe. "Did you ask her why she left in such a hurry?"

"Yep," said Jade. "And she acted like I was nuts! She was all like, 'What? I didn't leave in a hurry. It was just late, and I needed to get home.'"

"So she was defensive?" asked Cloe.

"Totally," replied Jade. Cloe and Jade sat and mulled over the information for a moment.

"I hate to say this," said Cloe, "but it really does seem like Kiana might have taken my purse. I just can't believe it. I mean, we're friends!"

"I know," said Jade. "It really bums me out that she would do that to you. And then try to hide it—it's so crazy!"

"What are we going to do?" asked Cloe. "Do we just come right out and ask her if she took it?"

"I don't think so," said Jade. "We have to play this carefully. There is still that teeny-tiny chance that it wasn't her."

"It's so complicated," said Cloe. "I don't even care about the purse. I just want that CD back!"

"Oh, wow!" Jade gasped, looking past Cloe at the entrance of the smoothie shop.

"What?" asked Cloe.

"You're not going to believe this, but Kiana just walked in!" Jade exclaimed.

"No way!" cried Cloe excitedly.

"Now we can get to the bottom of things!" whispered Jade.

"Oh my gosh, I'm so nervous," Cloe whispered back.

"Don't worry, I'll handle it," said Jade.

Kiana was in line to order her smoothie. She hadn't even acknowledged Cloe and Jade, even though there was no way she hadn't seen them—the smoothie shop was small, and they were sitting right by the door.

"Hey, Kiana!" yelled Jade. Cloe cringed, anxious about how Kiana would react. *Are we really about to bust Kiana right here in our fave smoothie shop?* she wondered.

Kiana acted like she hadn't heard Jade calling her, so this time Jade yelled a bit louder, "HEY, KIANA!"

Kiana turned around. She was smiling, but it was a nervous smile.

"Oh, hey, girls," she said. She approached them slowly. Cloe noticed that Kiana was fidgeting and her face was flushed. She was definitely on edge.

"Hey, girl," said Jade.

"Hey," said Kiana. She wouldn't look either of them in the eye.

"What's up?" asked Jade. "Just getting your smoothie fix?"

"Uh, yeah, I guess," stammered Kiana.

"What's your favorite kind?" asked Cloe. *What a lame question*, she thought. She was no good at this private detective stuff. She decided she would just leave it to Jade.

"Uh, mango pineapple?" Kiana answered uncertainly.

With a pointed glance at Cloe, Jade swiftly changed the subject. "So, did you have fun last night?" she asked cheerfully.

"Um, sure," replied Kiana.

"Wasn't Cameron's basement the perfect space for the party?" asked Jade. Then, without even waiting for an answer, she shot off more questions. *Kiana couldn't ignore all of them, could she?* "Did you like the decorations? Wasn't the music smokin'? Oh, and superdelish food, right? C'mon, Kiana, tell us what you really thought!"

"Um, it was all really great," said Kiana. "You guys did an awesome job. But I have to go. Sorry to take off, but there's that Spanish test tomorrow, you know . . ."

"You're so good at Spanish though," said Jade. "What are you worried about?"

But Kiana was already making her way toward the door. She was in such a rush that she didn't even bother to buy a smoothie on her way out.

"Bye, guys!" Kiana called over her shoulder, the door slamming shut behind her.

Cloe and Jade stared at each other in disbelief.

"Dude, she is so busted!" whispered Jade. "She was sweating bullets when I asked her about the party! It was crazy!"

"I know!" said Cloe, shaking her head. "She was turning green."

"That's it, she took it," said Jade. She sipped the last of her smoothie. "Case closed!"

"How should I confront her?" asked Cloe.

"Be direct. Tomorrow at school, just ask her why she's been acting so strangely, and hopefully she'll confess," said Jade.

Cloe knew Jade was right. But she still felt nervous about the whole thing. If Kiana *had* stolen her purse, how could she ever forgive her or trust her again? She would never feel totally safe around her. Just thinking about it made Cloe angry. But she also felt sad for Kiana. After all, what would make someone do something so awful? It was all so complicated.

"Hey listen, we better go," said Jade. "Now Kiana has me all nervous about the Spanish test, too! I have to get home and study."

"Good thinking," said Cloe.

As the girls gathered their things and moved toward the door, Cloe checked her cell phone. She had one message, but it was totally garbled. And when she checked her missed calls list, she found that the caller ID for that number was blocked.

"Do we know anyone with a blocked number?" Cloe asked Jade.

"Not that I can think of," Jade answered.

"I hate when that happens," Jade continued sympathetically. "Then I spend the next couple of hours racking my brain, trying to figure out who it could have been."

"Totally!" agreed Cloe.

"Well, they'll call back if it was important," said Jade.

"Yeah, you're probably right," said Cloe. "Good luck studying." She gave Jade a hug. "See you tomorrow."

Once she was outside, Cloe checked her voice mail again, but she still couldn't make out one word. She knew it was a little thing, but what with worrying about who had stolen her purse and stressing over trying to get Kiana to come clean, a mysterious phone call just felt like the last straw! Cloe was totally overwhelmed. She just hoped she would find answers to some of these questions soon.

Chapter 6

The next day at school, everyone had heard about Cloe's stolen purse. People had been supersweet all day, doling out sympathy and vowing to keep their eyes and ears open for any clues.

At lunch, Kiana ran up to Cloe. She was sitting at a table with Jade, Sasha, Yasmin, Cameron, Dylan, and Eitan. Kiana could barely get her words out—she was totally breathless.

"Cloe, oh my goodness, girl! I swore I saw your purse in the trash can by the gym!" she said.

"You did?" Cloe exclaimed incredulously.

"Totally! But ... then ... as I got closer, I realized it was just some gold wrapping paper."

"Well, thanks for trying," said Cloe, unable to conceal her disappointment. *Still, why would Kiana bring up the bag if she were the one who took it?* Cloe wondered. Was Kiana just trying to cover her tracks? Cloe decided she had to confront her right away. She figured it was the perfect opportunity, since Kiana had brought up the purse herself. Besides, Cloe knew she couldn't stand to stew over the whole situation one minute longer. She had to know the truth!

"Hey, Kiana, can I talk to you?" asked Cloe.

Kiana turned bright red. "Sure," she said.

"Let's take a walk," said Cloe. She got up

from the table and led Kiana out of the cafeteria and into the hallway. Cloe felt her stomach churning with anxiety. She had never had to do anything like this before!

Once they were in the hallway, Cloe just blurted it out. "Kiana, did you take my purse?" she asked.

"What?" Kiana cried, clearly offended.

"I'm so sorry to have to ask you like this, but it's just that you've been acting so nervous and shady ever since the party. I mean, until just now, you haven't looked any of us in the eye, and you totally avoid all questions about why you took off so quickly! I have a hard time believing you'd do something like that, but someone took my purse, and with how you've been behaving and all, you're kinda the prime suspect," explained Cloe. She felt awful having to accuse Kiana of something so terrible, but she really didn't know what else she could do.

Kiana took Cloe's hand. "Cloe, I'm so sorry I made you think that. I know I've been acting like a complete spaz. But I swear I didn't take your purse! I would never do that—especially to a good friend like you!"

"Then what's going on with you?" asked Cloe, still not sure whether to believe her or not. "And if you didn't take it, who did?"

"I really don't know who took your bag, but I think I can explain the way I've been acting," Kiana began.

"Go on," said Cloe.

"Okay, at the end of the party, right before I left, I was sipping my soda and having a great time. Then somebody bumped into me and I ended up spilling it all over Cameron's couch. I couldn't find any towels to clean up the mess, and I was so embarrassed about my klutziness that when I told Cameron about the stain, I left out the part about me being the one who had spilled the soda," explained Kiana.

"But then why were you hovering over by the closet for so long?" Cloe asked.

"Well, since I was one of the first people to leave the party, the closet was still completely packed with everybody's stuff and I had to dig around for a while before I found my coat."

Cloe felt terrible. It was obvious from

Kiana's genuine tone of voice that she was telling the truth. "There's no reason for you to be so embarrassed," Cloe said with a laugh. "We all have our klutzy moments—so what's a little spill among friends, right? Besides, since you told Cam about the stain right away, he was able to get it off. So it's really no biggie!"

"Oh my gosh, it's so good to hear you say that! I've been feeling so guilty about it—you have no idea!" said Kiana. "I'm definitely going to come clean to Cameron next."

"I'm glad you told me," said Cloe. "And I'm so sorry I accused you of stealing my purse. Now let's get some lunch. I'm starving!"

Cloe was relieved that Kiana wasn't the one who'd taken the bag. But as the two girls headed for the cafeteria, Cloe couldn't help feeling frustrated. She still had no idea who had taken it. Hopefully Jade would have a backup detective scheme!

As the girls approached the table, it was obvious that everyone was waiting for Kiana to confess.

"Guys, it wasn't Kiana," said Cloe. "It was a total mix-up. She was worried about something else." Cloe looked at Kiana and smiled. She didn't want to reveal Kiana's secret in front of everyone, especially since she knew how embarrassed Kiana had been.

"Are you sure?" asked Jade. She looked at Kiana accusingly.

"Positive," said Cloe.

"Okay then," said Jade. "But Kiana, you and I have to chat later—I've gotta hear why you were acting like such a weirdo!"

"Definitely, girl!" agreed Kiana. "It's totally silly, but don't worry, I'll give you the scoop." Jade and Kiana smiled at each other.

Cloe settled back into her seat beside Yasmin. "So if Kiana didn't do it, who did?" asked Yasmin anxiously.

"I don't know. But I'm not giving up until I have it figured out," Cloe vowed.

Chapter 7

After lunch, Cloe walked to her math class in a daze. No matter how hard she tried, she couldn't take her mind off the missing purse. The more she thought about it, the more spooked she got. It was just so creepy to think that someone had their hands on her personal belongings, and might have even listened to the CD she'd made especially for Cameron!

Cloe got to class just as her teacher, Mr. Gonzales, was beginning the lesson. "Good afternoon, math geniuses," he said. The class giggled uncomfortably. Mr. Gonzales was a great teacher, but he was kind of goofy. Math geniuses? As if!

Cloe tried to pay attention to Mr. Gonzales, but she couldn't focus. Her mind drifted as she tried to puzzle through who the thief might be. Suddenly, her thoughts were interrupted by a very loud voice calling her name.

"CLOE?"

She looked up, startled. Mr. Gonzales was staring at her expectantly. Cloe glanced around the room, confused and embarrassed.

"Uh . . ." she said. "I'm sorry, Mr. Gonzales, but what was the question?"

"If you'd been paying attention, you wouldn't have to ask," he scolded her.

"Oh . . . um . . . well . . ." Cloe squirmed

uncomfortably. "I'm sorry—I guess my mind just wandered."

"Please see me after class," Mr. Gonzales replied sternly before returning to the math problem on the board.

Cloe's cheeks went red with embarrassment, but she just nodded. She felt terrible. It wasn't like her to space out in class, but she was just feeling so overwhelmed lately.

When the bell rang, she gathered her books and timidly approached Mr. Gonzales's desk. "Hi, Mr. Gonzales," she said meekly. "Listen, I am so sorry for spacing in class today."

"Cloe," Mr. Gonzales replied, concerned, "is everything okay? It's not like you to be so distracted in class."

"I know, and I apologize. I've just been, well, dealing with some stuff lately," said Cloe. "But I know that's no excuse, and I'm really sorry."

"Is everything okay at home?" asked Mr. Gonzales.

"Oh no, it's nothing like that," said Cloe. "See, it's sort of silly actually. I mean, in comparison to people with real problems and stuff."

"If it's really bothering you, Cloe, then it isn't silly," he said. "Do you want to talk about it? This is my free period, so I have some time. And don't worry about being late to your next class— I'd be happy to write you a pass if you want."

Cloe sat down. Maybe it would be good to talk the situation over with someone older who she respected. "It's just that this past weekend my purse was stolen and, well, I just can't shake it. It's really got me upset."

"Oh, Cloe, that's tough," said Mr. Gonzales sympathetically. "I'm sorry to hear that happened to you."

"Yeah, thanks," said Cloe.

"Do you have any idea who might have taken it?" asked Mr. Gonzales.

"No, I really have no clue," replied Cloe.

"Do you want my advice?" asked Mr. Gonzales.

"Actually, yeah, I'd really appreciate it," said Cloe.

"My advice is to try as hard as you can to push this out of your mind. I know it's not easy, but if the bag really was stolen, there's not much you can do at this point. The best thing you can do is keep in mind that if someone was desperate enough to steal your purse, maybe they needed it more than you did. That doesn't make it okay, of course, but maybe it will make you feel a little better about the whole thing."

Cloe nodded—he had a good point. Mr. Gonzales continued, "On the other hand, if it was taken accidentally, you have to trust that whoever did it will own up to their mistake and return your bag. I know it's tough, but you need to try to take as positive a view as possible, for your own peace of mind."

"Thank you, Mr. Gonzales. I totally get what you're saying," said Cloe.

"I'm glad," said Mr. Gonzales. "I have a lot

of faith in you, Cloe. I'm so sorry this happened to you, but you're a strong young lady, and I know you'll get through it with flying colors."

"Thanks," replied Cloe. "That helps a lot. I guess I better get to my next class. Thanks for everything, seriously."

"Glad to be of service," said Mr. Gonzales, giving her a silly little salute as he handed her a hall pass. "Keep your chin up! And no more space-cadet stuff in class!" he called after her.

"No more, I swear!" Cloe replied, waving cheerfully over her shoulder.

Chapter 8

Cloe's next class was gym, and she was really looking forward to sweating off her worries. Today they were playing volleyball, one of her favorite sports. She changed into her gym clothes and took her place on the court. Each time the ball came over the net, she returned it effortlessly.

"Angel, you are on *fire* today!" yelled Sasha.

Cloe smiled. It felt so great to be out on the court, moving and sweating and focusing on the game rather than on her missing purse.

At the end of the game, Cloe got tons of praise from everybody on her team. "Cloe, wow!"

said Oriana. "You really served it up out there!"

Cloe laughed. "Yeah," she said. "I guess I'm taking out my anger on the ball."

"Oh, yeah, I heard about your purse," Oriana replied. "I can't believe somebody would steal from you."

"Yeah, I know," Cloe said with a sigh. "It's totally wack, but what can I do?"

"Well, hopefully it'll turn up, and it'll be like the whole thing never happened," said Oriana.

"Thanks, Oriana," said Cloe as they walked to the locker room to shower and change.

Cloe saw Sasha and Jade waiting for her at her locker. "Hey, what are you doing after school?" Sasha asked as they all opened their lockers.

"Not too much," said Cloe. "I might cruise

to the mall to find a purse replacement."

"Really? Well, maybe I'll go with you," said Sasha as she opened her locker. She swiveled to retrieve her things and let out a gasp.

"Sasha, what's the matter?" asked Cloe.

Sasha did a double take and pulled the locker door back to check the number.

"You guys!" she whispered. "This locker was unlocked, and I opened it by mistake! You've got to come look . . ." Sasha glanced around furtively. She motioned Cloe and Jade to come closer and pulled the door back to reveal the locker's contents to them both.

Cloe gasped too. There, in the locker, was her missing purse!

Chapter 9

The girls looked at one another, mouths open. No one knew what to say. Just then, they heard someone come up behind them. Cloe turned around and saw Valentina.

Valentina's eyes were downcast. She couldn't look any of them in the face. Cloe, Jade, and Sasha just stood still, waiting for her to speak.

"That's my locker," Valentina said meekly. She looked like she was going to cry.

"Oh yeah?" said Sasha. "That's funny. Because if it's your locker, then what's Cloe's purse doing inside of it?"

"Listen, I can explain!" Valentina replied as her eyes welled up and her voice quivered with emotion. "I've been trying to talk to you all day, Cloe, I swear. But I was just so embarrassed!"

"What do you mean, *embarrassed*?" Jade answered coldly. "Embarrassed that you're a thief?"

"No, that's not it, I swear," said Valentina. "Please, guys, just let me explain."

"Okay, so explain," replied Sasha.

"Okay, so at Cameron's party I was having so much fun," Valentina began.

"Having fun stealing?" snapped Jade.

"Come on, you two, it's okay," said Cloe. Even though she was angry and confused, Cloe knew that Valentina deserved to tell her side of the story— and that Jade and Sasha were too upset to really listen. "In fact, why don't I catch up with you?" she suggested to her friends. "Give Valentina a chance to explain, one-on-one."

"If that's what you want," Sasha said. Jade shrugged in agreement. As they gathered their stuff to go, they glanced at Cloe to make sure she was really okay. When she gave them a reassuring nod, they headed out, both mouthing "Call me later!" as they left the locker room.

Once they were alone, Valentina smiled at Cloe gratefully. "So like I was saying, it really was the best party ever. And I was totally having a blast, laughing and dancing and all. So when it was time to leave, I just grabbed my jacket and what I thought was my bag. But the thing was, I was so caught up in everything that I totally spaced on the fact that I hadn't even brought my purse to the party!" explained Valentina.

"Wait, so let me get this straight," replied Cloe. "You're saying you have a purse just like mine?"

"Yes! I got it last week at Etc.!" Valentina exclaimed.

That was where Cloe had bought her purse, too, so Valentina's story made sense.

"Anyway, when I got home I realized that my purse was on my bed, right where I'd left it. I panicked and looked inside the bag and it was yours, Cloe! I was so embarrassed that I'd made such a silly mistake," Valentina confessed.

"But why didn't you just call me?" Cloe asked.

"I did call you!" said Valentina. "I called you on Sunday morning and left a message, but you never called me back."

"Wait, does your number come up as an unknown ID?" asked Cloe.

"Yeah, that's how my home number comes up," said Valentina.

"I got your message," said Cloe. "The thing is, it was completely garbled and I couldn't hear any of it! I replayed it a couple of times, but I couldn't make out one word."

"That explains it," said Valentina. "I was convinced that you hadn't called me back because you hated me for being so stupid! My plan was to return your purse first thing this morning, Cloe, I swear. But when I tried, I just felt so shy about it. Especially since I kept it so long, you know? I was scared you wouldn't buy my story."

Valentina pulled the purse out of her locker and handed it to Cloe. "Here you go," said Valentina. "I am really, truly so sorry for everything."

Cloe opened the bag, and everything was still inside it, just as she had left it—including the CD she had made for Cameron!

She smiled at Valentina. "It's all right. I just wish you would have talked to me sooner," said Cloe.

"Thank you so much for believing me, Cloe," said Valentina appreciatively.

"But you know it has to be the truth—I mean, could I make up something so lame if I tried?"

"Probably not," Cloe agreed, giggling.

"I hope you can forgive me," Valentina said.

"Definitely!" Cloe said. "Besides, how could I hold a grudge against someone with the same supreme fashion sense as me?" Valentina laughed, and the girls shared a hug.

"I couldn't help but notice that smokin' CD," Valentina added shyly. "Did you make that yourself?"

"Yeah, I did," said Cloe, pleased that Valentina was giving her props. "I made it for Cameron . . . for his birthday."

"You did?" cried Valentina. "That is so cool. What a fantastic friend you are!"

"Thanks," Cloe said. "It was supposed to be a surprise. I was planning to give it to him after the party, but then, well, you know . . ."

"Your purse was nowhere to be found!" Valentina chimed in. "Aw, geez, now I really feel terrible about making such a huge mistake. I just hope I didn't ruin his birthday! If only I'd looked in the bag before I left and had seen that it wasn't mine, this whole mess could have been avoided."

"No, it's okay, don't beat yourself up about it," replied Cloe. "Everyone makes mistakes, including me—like, all the time!"

Cloe shut her locker, ready to go home.

"So, are you gonna give Cameron the CD now?" Valentina asked.

Cloe was so happy to have her purse back

that she hadn't even thought about it. *How fun!* she thought. Now that she had the gift she'd promised Cameron back in her hands, she could *really* surprise him with it! "Yeah! Totally!" she replied.

"He's definitely going to love it," said Valentina.

Cloe glanced at her watch. This was their last class of the day, and she only had a little bit of time to find Cameron before he left for the day.

"Oh wow, I better go if I'm gonna catch him before he jets. Thanks again, Valentina. I really appreciate that you came clean."

"No, thank *you* for being so completely cool and understanding," replied Valentina. "And good luck with Cameron—I know he's gonna love it!"

Chapter 10

Cloe wove through the crowded halls, on the lookout for Cameron. Suddenly she spotted him standing at his locker.

"Cameron!" yelled Cloe.

Cameron turned, looking expectantly for whoever was calling his name. When his eyes settled on Cloe, he broke into a big smile.

"Hey, Cloe, what's up?" asked Cameron.

"Guess what?" said Cloe excitedly.

"What?" asked Cameron.

"I got my purse back!" Cloe exclaimed.

"Are you serious?" said Cameron, grinning

broadly. "That's so great! How did it happen?"

Cloe told Cameron the whole story. When she finished, Cameron shook his head in disbelief.

"That's a crazy story, but I'm just psyched that you have your bag back," he said. "You have no idea how much that bummed me out. To think that someone would steal from you in my house was just too much, man."

"I know, it was terrible," said Cloe. "And I really appreciate your support—all of you guys were so sweet to me throughout this whole drama."

"Cloe, it was no problem at all," said Cameron. "We care about you, and if something bad happens to you, then it happens to all of us."

"Thanks, Cam," said Cloe. "But listen, enough about the bag. Remember when I told you I had a present for you at your party?"

Cameron grinned. "Oh, yeah, right before we discovered that your bag was missing."

"Exactly," said Cloe. "See, your present was in my purse. So not only was my purse gone, but so was your present! That's a big part of why I was upset," she explained. "But now that I have my purse back, you get your present!"

"Sweet!" said Cameron. He couldn't wait to find out what it was—Cloe's excitement was contagious.

"Okay, here it is," said Cloe. She reached inside her bag to retrieve the CD and nervously handed it to Cameron. "Happy birthday,

Cameron," she said meekly. She couldn't believe how nervous she was! She really hoped that he would like it.

"Oh wow," said Cameron. He looked at the specially designed case. "This case is so fly! Cloe, did you make this yourself?"

"Yeah," Cloe replied shyly.

"It's so creative and cool. And this playlist!" he exclaimed as he flipped the case over to read the back. "It's seriously all of my favorite tunes! I mean really, this gift is amazing. It means so much to me that you would spend so much time on something for me!"

"I'm so glad you like it!" exclaimed Cloe. Even though she had been pretty sure that Cameron would like the CD, she still felt relieved to hear him say so.

"Are you kidding?" asked Cameron. "It's the best gift ever. I can't wait to play it. Do you want to come back to my house and listen to it with me?"

"Oh, I totally would," said Cloe, "except that I have to call my girls and fill them in on what happened!"

"Oh, yeah, I bet," said Cameron, laughing. "They're gonna flip!"

"Totally!" agreed Cloe. "Yasmin doesn't even know what happened yet. And Sasha and Jade were there when we found the purse, but they still don't know how it turned out. I'm going to take them out for smoothies to celebrate my purse's return!"

"Okay, then I'll call you as soon as I listen to

the CD," said Cameron. "And thanks again for such an awesome present! You're the coolest!"

Cloe laughed and waved good-bye. The purse had been found, Cameron had gotten his present at last, and she was on her way to hang out with her favorite people on the planet—Jade, Sasha, and Yasmin.

Things were looking up for sure!